For Sebastian

—E.C.

Illustrations executed in gouache and pen and ink on Lanaquarelle hot-press watercolor paper.
Text is 15/21-point Century Oldstyle.

ISBN 0-590-51185-8

20 19 18 17 16 15 14 13   1 2/0

Printed in the U.S.A.   08

First Scholastic printing, February 1999

Five Little Monkeys With Nothing To Do

Written and Illustrated by Eileen Christelow

SCHOLASTIC INC.

New York Toronto London Auckland Sydney
Mexico City New Delhi Hong Kong

It is summer. There is no school.
Five little monkeys tell their mama,
"We're bored. There is nothing to do!"
"Oh yes there is," says Mama.
"Grandma Bessie is coming for lunch,
and the house must be neat and clean.

"So . . . you can pick up your room."

9

Five little monkeys pick up and pick up and pick up . . .

. . . until everything is put away.

"Good job!" says Mama.
"But we're bored again,"
say five little monkeys.
"There is nothing to do!"
"Oh yes there is," says Mama.
"You can scrub the bathroom.
The house must be neat and clean
for Grandma Bessie."

So five little monkeys scrub and scrub and scrub until the bathroom shines.

"Good job!" says Mama.
    "But we're bored again,"
say five little monkeys.
"There is nothing to do!"
    "Oh yes there is," says Mama.
"You can beat the dirt out of these rugs.
The house must be neat and clean
for Grandma Bessie."

Five little monkeys beat and beat and beat the rugs
until there is not a speck of dirt left.

"Good job!" says Mama.
"But we're bored again," say five little monkeys.
"There is nothing to do!"

"Oh yes there is," says Mama.
"You can pick some berries down by the swamp.
Grandma Bessie loves berries for dessert."

Five little monkeys run down
to the muddy, muddy swamp.

They pick and pick and pick berries
until Mama calls, "It's time to come home!"

Five little monkeys run inside
while Mama picks flowers.
"Put the berries in the kitchen,"
calls Mama. "Wash your faces
and put on clean clothes."

Five little monkeys wash their faces . . .

. . . and they put on clean clothes.
"Grandma Bessie is here!" calls Mama.

Five little monkeys race outside.

They hug and kiss Grandma Bessie.
"We've been busy all day!" they say.
"We cleaned the house and picked berries
just for you!"

"I love berries," says Grandma Bessie.
"And I love a clean house, too!"

They all go inside.

"Oh my!" says Grandma Bessie.
"Oh dear!" says Mama.
"Oh no!" say five little monkeys.
"Who messed up our nice, clean house?"

"I can't imagine," says Mama.
"But whoever did has plenty to do!"